7/12/08

KENDALL & KENNETH

Enjoy the

NEW ADVENTURE!

Uncle E

"BOOGIE AND THE BUBBLES"

Written by: Uncle E
Illustrated by: Sash

W3 Publishing

A division of Kellum Enterprises, LLC

PO Box 1255 Suitland, MD 20752

Book design by Sash Productions

Summary: Boogie baits her brother, Diggle, to play a competitive game with her involving some bubbles that they have not been given permission to access. An unexpected adventure comes from this bubble play that causes the two siblings to learn a lesson in obedience (story written in rhyme).

ISBN 978-0-9801322-2-9

For retail orders please check us out at dbladventures.com or diggleboogieandlolo.com

For bulk orders please email: info@dbladventures.com

Printed in China by Diya USA

1st Edition

To Susan Elizabeth

Let me be clear-

The kids are great! I like them alot ☺

Thanks for them!

...But there is no one in this world that I love more than you.

NEVER forget that!

Oh, and Symone, WELCOME TO THE FAMILY!

Your book will be coming soon!

Hi! I'm Taylor,
but my daddy calls me **Boogie.**
I'm Eric's little sister,
but that don't mean I'm a rookie.
Eric is my big brother.
He's seven, so he's older.
But I'm four and getting bigger.
Why... I already come past his shoulder.

My daddy calls Eric, **Diggle.**
And we have a baby sister, **LoLo.**
LoLo grabs her coat alot.
She's always yelling "go go".

Diggle's really smart.
He learns alot in school.
He plays a lot of sports,
and he thinks reading is cool.

My siblings really love me!
...I guess I love them, too.
And my daddy says he can write
a lot of books on all the things that we go
through.

He says we are like normal kids,
but we do really abnormal things...
like soaking our feet in toilet bowls
or "shaving" our faces with diaper cream.

My dad says it's always an adventure
when his three kids are on the go so
sit back and take things slow so
that you enjoy...

One day,
Diggle and Boogie were playing a game of hide and go seek.
"READY OR NOT...HERE I COME!" Diggle did loudly speak.
It was usually easy to find Boogie;
her hiding was not discreet.
Diggle would normally hear her laughing,
or hear the floor underneath her creek.

It would only take seconds for Diggle to find Boogie
ANY day of the week.
But this day seemed different...
as if Diggle was ending his *finding hiding Boogie streak.*

Boy, things were looking bleak.
He searched all the Boogie hiding places:
her room, her closet, the bathtub and
all the storage spaces.
He checked the playroom, the guest room,
the kitchen, his room, their parents room, the den...

...he got so frustrated because he couldn't find her,
that he checked all those places again.

"WHERE COULD BOOGIE BE?!" thought Diggle.
He was getting bothered.
But Diggle wasn't the only one looking for Boogie.
He heard his mommy holler,
"TAYLOR!!!!!!!!"

(Now let's stop right here to quickly explain
Diggle's sister is called Boogie, but Taylor is her real name.
And when Mommy calls the *real names*, things are not the same.
That means Mommy is very serious and not in the mood for games.)

"TAYLOR, FOR SHAME," Mommy exclaimed; she sounded consumed.
Diggle followed the frustrated voice till it led him to the laundry room.
When he got there, he realized why Boogie was a good hider.
There was Mommy, very upset...pulling Boogie out of the dryer!

"You are NOT to hide in the dryer!" an upset Mommy said to Boogie, who had pants on her shoulders and a sock on top of her head.

"I was playing hide and seek," said Boogie. "This is where I hid today."

"I told you before 'NO DRYER HIDING'," Mommy reminded. "And I mean just what I say!"

Mommy took Boogie away.
Their exit was expedient.
"Taylor, how many times do I say this?
You have got to be obedient!
You must obey your parents, even if
you don't agree yourself.
Because if you disobey,
one day,
you'll hurt yourself...
or someone else."

Mommy put Boogie in the corner...for five minutes...she had a time out.
Diggle had no one to play with...for five minutes...he took a dime out,
and began spinning it on the floor; he must have spun the time away.
Before he knew it, there was Boogie saying,
"Hey Diggle, you ready to play?"

They ran back up the stairs
to find a new game on the double.
"Oh, I know what we can play," said Boogie.
"Let's open the bottles of bubbles."

"But Mommy said *not* to open them," Diggle reminded. "Until she gave permission."
But Boogie continued to open them; she pretended not to listen.
Diggle just stood there, watching Boogie blow the bubbles.
He was determined not to play; he didn't want to get in trouble.

But then Boogie made a BIG BUBBLE...
bigger than any that Diggle had done.
"I bet you can't make one bigger," Boogie boasted.
Diggle thought, "It wouldn't hurt if I made just one."

Diggle made a bigger bubble.
Then Boogie made one bigger than that.
Diggle had to make another one
just so he could add better bigger bubbles
to his collection of *big brother stats*.

They went on for twenty minutes with this big bubble competition.
By then, the floor was wet with water and needed intervention.
They put the bottles on the table and checked for towels in the kitchen.
Returning to fix their mess was their original intention.
"I found the towels," said Diggle, ready to complete their cleaning mission.
But as they were leaving the kitchen,
a familiar voice caught their attention.

"Your favorite heroes are in trouble, and need your help, kids... BELIEVE ME!"
They looked up and saw HeroBoy and She-RoGirl playing on the TV.
It was an interactive episode that they had never seen before.
They postponed drying the floor... their heroes needed them more.

Now while they were intensely watching their favorite Hero Show,
someone spotted the bubbles!
That someone was none other than...
...Lo!
Diggle and Boogie were so into the show, they didn't even blink...
There was LoLo, alone with the bubbles, as she mumbled, "LoLo Drink!"

LoLo opened the bottle and quickly took a sip.
Then she let out a burp with bubbles forming from her lips.
LoLo liked the effect, so she started to do it again.
But she was startled when she heard,
"NO LOLO" coming from the den.

LoLo dropped the bottle of bubbles,
which made a larger puddle.
Daddy left the den to rescue LoLo on the double.
LoLo cried out, "Daah", with residue of more bubbles.
Daddy hurried to rescue his daughter...then things really got muddled.

You see, Daddy was running so fast that he couldn't control his pace.
He stepped onto the puddle, then he slipped and hit his face.
He had built so much momentum, that he didn't stop right there.
He slid past LoLo,
the puddle,
the bubbles...all the way down a flight of stairs!

Diggle and Boogie went to investigate the noise that they just heard.
They found Daddy lying at the bottom of the stairs, but he didn't say a word.
With one hand he held his hip.
With the other he held his head.
This scenario was serenaded with silence until Boogie concluded, "Daddy's dead."

"Daddy's not dead," said Diggle.
"He just hurt himself when he slid."
Then Diggle and Boogie looked at each other.
Could he have slid because of what they did?
Could he have hurt himself because they were playing with bubbles?
"What's going on out there?" Mommy shouted.
LoLo warned them, "Oooh, look like tubble."

Diggle and Boogie acted quickly.
The bubbles they had to rid.
And while Daddy was lying there,
before Mommy came out,
they ran to Diggle's room and hid...

They hid in the closet by Diggle's shoes.
Inside them were a pair of socks.
"Diggle, do you think we're safe?" asked Boogie.
Just then they heard a knock.
"Eric and Taylor!" exclaimed Mommy, "I need you to appear."
There was silence for two seconds...
Then Boogie blurted, "NOBODY'S HERE!"

"Boogie! What are you doing!" Diggle was confiding.
"You've got to do a better job of not making noise when you're hiding."
At that moment, Diggle and Boogie heard the opening of Diggle's door.
And at the sound of footsteps,
Boogie said, "I don't want to hide here anymore."
"Eric and Taylor Kelsey!" demanded Mommy.
"I will not say this again.
You will come out of this closet RIGHT NOW...
OR ELSE - I'm coming in!"

At the sound of that warning,
the kids opened the closet door.
"Oh, hey Mommy," said Diggle.
"We were just...
cleaning the closet floor".

At that moment, Daddy walked in for the surprise family meeting. He had a bandage on his head so that he could stop the bleeding. LoLo was in his arms. She saw here siblings and said, "Uh Oh...Dig and Boog in tubble".

"Yes, you are in trouble," Mommy quickly agreed. "And a result for your disobedience is exactly what you need."

"But your daughter started it," pleaded Diggle.
"She opened up the bottle."
Boogie looked at her brother with a look that was quite hostile.

"It doesn't matter who started it," Mommy then explained.
"Both of you contributed to the cause of your Daddy's pain.
Have I instructed you not to open the bottles without permission?
Were you disobedient? Did you make your own decision?"

"Yes, we were disobedient," Diggle and Boogie did confess.
Boogie added, "We just wanted to play the bigger bubble contest."

Mommy said, "I'm sorry, kids. That excuse is very sad.
It would have only taken seconds to go ask your mom or dad.
But you didn't feel like asking, and that makes me very mad...
not at you,
but the truth is...
your actions hurt your dad really bad.
You must obey your parents, even if you don't agree yourself.
Because when you disobey,
you hurt yourself or someone else."

After Mommy's words, Boogie had something to say...
"Daddy, we're really sorry we hurt you today."

Daddy said, "I forgive you. I love you, anyway...
...but disobedience costs, and I'm afraid you have to pay."

That day,
Diggle and Boogie had lessons of obedience on their minds.
They also had some lessons instilled on their behinds.
They also cleaned up the mess from the bubble blowing bash,
and they helped to nurse their father from the sliding daddy crash.
And hopefully their memory will flash back to what their mommy had to say:

"Disobedience hurts you and others,
SO DON'T DISOBEY!"

The End

About the Author- Uncle E is a poet, storyteller, and father of three wonderful children. These wonderful children have allowed him to witness so many adventures, that he figured he could write books about them. He has been working in the community with youth and families for over 10 years. He currently lives in Suitland, Maryland with his beautiful wife of 9 years, those three adventurous children, AND baby Symone, the newest addition of the family, who will have her own book series one day. ☺

About the Artist- Steven "Sash" Scott, of Bowie Maryland, was the orginal illustrator for GIRL'S LIFE magazine's *Penny Lane*. He has painted many murals in Washington D.C. and is currently the writer and artist of the URBAN PROTECTORS found at **www.sovereign-pictures.com**

For more information about upcoming DBL books, please visit

DBLadventures.com

or

diggleboogieandlolo.com